The
Waters
& the
Wild

Also by Francesca Lia Block

WEETZIE BAT

GIRL GODDESS #9: NINE STORIES

THE HANGED MAN

DANGEROUS ANGELS: THE WEETZIE BAT BOOKS

I WAS A TEENAGE FAIRY

VIOLET & CLAIRE

THE ROSE AND THE BEAST

ECHO

GUARDING THE MOON

WASTELAND

GOAT GIRLS: TWO WEETZIE BAT BOOKS

BEAUTIFUL BOYS: TWO WEETZIE BAT BOOKS

NECKLACE OF KISSES

PSYCHE IN A DRESS

BLOOD ROSES

HOW TO (UN)CAGE A GIRL

The Waters & the Wild

FRANCESCA LIA BLOCK

HARPER TEEN
An Imprint of HarperCollins*Publishers*

The title of this book is inspired by William Butler Yeats's poem "The Stolen Child," excerpted on p. 69.

HarperTeen is an imprint of HarperCollins Publishers.

The Waters & the Wild

Library of Congress Cataloging-in-Publication Data
Block, Francesca Lia.
    The waters & the wild / Francesca Lia Block. — 1st ed.
        p.   cm.
    Summary: Thirteen-year-old Bee realizes that she is a fairy who has been switched at birth with another girl who now wants her life back.
    ISBN 978-0-06-145244-4 (trade bdg.)
    ISBN 978-0-06-145245-1 (lib. bdg.)
    [1. Changelings—Fiction.   2. Schools—Fiction.   3. Los Angeles (Calif.)—Fiction.]   I. Title.
PZ7.B61945Wat   2009   2008031452
[Fic]—dc22   CIP
                                                                 AC

09 10 11 12 13   LP/RRDB   10 9 8 7 6 5 4 3 2 1
❖
First Edition

THANKS TO
GILDA BLOCK, LYDIA WILLS,
TARA WEIKUM, JOCELYN DAVIES,
ALYSSA REUBEN, JASON YARN,
AND LAURA KAPLAN .

AND TO MY READERS,
MY CONSTANT INSPIRATION

FOR MY CHANGELINGS

The seasons alter . . .

And this same progeny of evils comes

From our debate, from our dissension;

We are their parents and original.

—William Shakespeare, *A Midsummer Night's Dream*

thirteen ways to know you are a changeling

1. you have never felt as if you quite belonged
2. when you love someone it is like immolation or drowning
3. you yearn for the earth, even fantasize about eating it in handfuls
4. your skin does not seem like your own
5. metal frightens you
6. light on shallow water causes you to gasp
7. as do the carcasses of sea lions prepared by taxidermists for the coldly lit cases of dark museums

8. touch is one of the only ways you know to get back to yourself

9. but with the wrong human it can take you farther and farther away until you almost cease to exist

10. you have repeated dreams of flying even though it takes tremendous effort and feels more like running a race

11. you have abandonment issues without necessarily any obvious cause

12. you are always secretly seeking ways to hurt yourself, as if this might prove to whoever is in charge that your tasks are done

13. hopefully, when you are young you discover something called love, which is really just another name for going home

Haze

When Bee woke up, there was a girl standing in her room.

"You are me," the girl said.

Then she was gone.

The eucalyptus leaves, rung by the night breeze, tinkled as if the salt from the sea air had crystallized, turned them to glass. Bee got out of bed, flung herself to the window and looked out at the sleeping garden. The polished glass chips in the flower beds and the sequins on the saris hanging over the gazebo reflected the light of the full spring moon and made the air phosphorescent.

But there was not even the shadow of a girl.

The loneliness Bee always felt—had felt since she could remember feeling anything at all—was so big now, so alive, that it was almost a creature. And after what she had seen, it felt colder, crueler than ever.

As a little girl she couldn't make friends. She was too quiet, unable to read. Her teachers thought she had a learning disability, and for a while she was in Occupational Therapy trying to learn how to interpret facial expressions and the tones of people's voices. Now she struggled through school, just passing every semester.

"You're smart," her mother said. "It has nothing to do with intelligence. Some of the most creative minds were diagnosed with learning disabilities."

School wasn't the only problem. Even with the O.T. it was hard to know how to act with people. And everything about Bee was odd. She couldn't eat animal flesh or watch all that television, try to talk about what celebrities were wearing or the war in Iraq. She preferred the solitude of her mother's garden.

"Miss Green Thumb," her mom called her. When she was little she fantasized about eating handfuls of dirt to be closer to nature. The red, yellow and sterling roses bloomed bigger than cupcakes. The water hyacinth in the pond burst into edible-looking purple-and-white blossoms. As she got older she tended that pond, lovingly, feeding the koi, gently lifting out the plants with their long trailing roots to clean the filter, drain and refill the water. On the mossy bank by the pool she set out rose-petal beds and an abalone-shell bath, filled with water that brought out its rainbows. She squeezed lemons from the tree and picked figs, made lemonade and fig cakes in tiny cupcake holders, put them out on doll-house china. In the morning the food was gone and the beds looked slept in.

That is the world I belong in, she thought. The tiny garden world. Not this.

Ever since she was a small child, Bee knew she couldn't tell her mom about the mystery in the garden. Now she had another secret: the girl in her room. Deena didn't believe in the supernatural. She was a born scientist; everything had a tangible cause, related to some function of the brain. But for Bee this way of looking at the world felt empty, as if you were trying to explain away angels as static in the temporal lobe, deities as no more than electricity.

Joseph Hayes, or "Haze," as they called him. He might know something about all of this. He always had a book with him, and those thick glasses to hide behind. People said he thought he was an alien. After last night she would have believed almost anything.

Haze was sitting alone as usual at lunchtime. She slid onto the chair across from him. He glanced up. She hadn't noticed his eyes before, with those glasses and all. But they were huge and dark, and even this far across the table she thought she saw herself reflected in them like two little dolls.

She thought, He's weird, in a good way. Weird like me.

He was reading his book. It was a withered old volume, leather-bound. It looked ancient but preserved, like a mummy inside its linen binding. Bee wondered what it was about.

"Hello," she said.

He seemed startled that she would sit here at all, let alone talk to him. They said he stuttered, but she'd never heard him speak once. Not that she talked much herself, but her life had changed overnight.

"I'm Bee."

He nodded. He had high, fine cheekbones

and lips like a starlet's. A little acne on his high forehead where a black lock of hair fell forward over his eyes.

Haze. Who was this boy? Everyone made fun of him. He stammered. He was smart. Unironically ugly, thick-lensed, thick-framed glasses. Problem skin. Beautiful eyes. Hands with tapered fingers and prominent veins, although his nails were bitten so much it looked painful. He had nice lips. Did anyone notice those lips? Did he really believe he was an alien? He read big thick books about stuff most people didn't believe existed.

"You're Haze, right?"

He nodded again, looked down at his book.

"What are you reading?"

He closed and turned it so she could see the cover.

The Encyclopedia of the Paranormal. She knew he was the right one to talk to.

"I have a question for you and your book."

This sparked his interest, she could tell. His eyes got darker behind the lenses of his glasses and he tilted his head almost imperceptibly to the side, watching her. She realized he hadn't said a word this whole time, but it felt like he had, somehow.

"Is there some phenomenon about someone who looks just like you, like a twin? What's that called? This twin who shows up and then just disappears?"

He was finding something in his book, flipping through it—he knew what he wanted. Yes, there it was. He pushed it across the table to her.

"Doppelganger," it said.

She read the definition. A chill grazed her spine, as if he'd slipped an ice cube down her shirt. But Haze would never have done that. He wasn't a tease. He wasn't a flirt. And the chill was worse, too, than ice. So cold it went through her skin and penetrated to the marrow of her bones.

She read further. "The sighting of one's doppelganger is often associated with a premonition of the viewer's imminent death."

> " 'Ere Babylon was dust,
> The Magus Zoroaster, my dead child,
> Met his own image walking in the garden.
> That apparition, sole of men, he saw.
> For know there are two worlds of life and
>   death:
> One that which thou beholdest; but the other
> Is underneath the grave, where do inhabit

The shadows of all forms that think and live
Till death unite them and they part no more . . .'"

"What?" The words were like a cold, bitter-sweet elixir that made her spine tingle. "Who wrote that?" she asked, but it was suddenly hard to talk.

"Sh-helley," Haze stammered. His voice, quoting the poem, had been like ironed silk or still water. "We all die, though, you know? It isn't that bad really."

She got up from the table. The cafeteria floor was so sticky that her sneakers made a soft popping when she moved; it sounded as if someone was following her. All around her was noise and the sickening smells of grease. Her stomach tumbled, nauseous, and the faces of the other kids eating their lunches glowed with a bilious yellow-greenish light, the color of fear. Why had she talked to him at all?

"Wait."

But she was hurrying away from him. In the glass cafeteria wall a girl was running beside her.

2

Identity Thing

Lew was in the garden, under the plum tree, when she got home from school. Doing some-one's chart. As practical as her mom was, Lew was the opposite. Just dreaming all the time. Making a living from astrology and tarot read-ings, publishing the occasional esoteric article. He pushed his wheelchair back from the table when she got there. There were purple plum stains on the brick patio.

"Are you okay?" she asked him.

"I was just going to ask you that."

"You look pale."

"So do you. Did you eat?"

"I don't have much appetite. It was a rough night."

"Bad dreams?"

Lew was watching her carefully now. He did look pale. She wondered how much pain he was in all the time, pretending he wasn't. A pale bluish halo of light surrounded his gray hair.

"What does that mean?" he asked.

She wanted to confide in him. She needed to talk to someone and he would understand better than her mom would, but it was difficult for her to say it.

Finally she blurted out, "What do you know about doppelgangers?"

"Supposedly Abraham Lincoln saw one. And Percy Shelley. John Donne. Your mom thinks it's related to stress. They were all ill, under stress at the time. John Donne's wife had a stillborn baby. I don't know much more. That's from Wikipedia."

She sat down on the grass and started pulling the heads off of the little daisies that bordered the wall of bougainvillea. Crushing them in her fingers until they felt wet, like with blood; tossing them aside.

"Why? What's wrong? Too much stress at school?"

She shook her head. "I don't fit in. So boring. Every teenager feels like that."

"That doesn't mean it's easy."

Really, she didn't believe that she felt like

every teenager at all. She was much more of a freak. Than anyone, probably, except maybe Haze.

"I had an experience," Bee said. It was a risk to tell Lew. He might tell her mom. But she couldn't hold it back anymore.

"Do you think this is something for your mother? Is it about boys?"

She grimaced. "No. Not that. Don't worry."

"Okay, sorry. Tell me, kiddo."

"I saw someone in my room last night."

Lew jerked forward so abruptly she was afraid he'd fall.

"A girl," she added.

"In your room?"

"She looked just like me."

"So that's what this doppelganger talk is about."

"Yes, well. I don't know. She was just standing there, and then she said, 'You are me,' and disappeared. I didn't dream it."

"'You are me'? What do you think it's about?"

"I have no idea. Mom would say it's a hallucination. Too much stress, like you said. Don't tell her."

"Well, you are our little Gemini after all."

"Very funny. So says the astrologer."

"No, I mean seriously, from a symbology perspective. Let's say she wasn't a real girl. What do you think the significance is? Is it about growing up?"

"What does that mean?"

"An identity thing. 'You are me.' Leaving one self behind for a new one. But the old self is always part of you, too. Does that sound right?"

"No. I don't know."

"Who are you, then?"

She scowled at him. Even if she pretended (I am a thirteen-year-old double Gemini girl—Scorpio moon—who lives with her therapist mom and her mom's astrologer boyfriend in Venice, California; I go to school, where I get bad grades; I write poetry with my left hand, dance in my room, read books, listen to music, Google images of goblins and the tattoos my mom won't let me get, dream of devouring my garden), she really had no idea.

In some ways that was nearly as frightening as seeing the girl in her room.

"Some people think you begin to grow up when you stop trying to figure out who you are," Lew said.

3

Strange Fruit

The girl was singing to herself under the jacaranda tree, her eyes looking skyward and her full mouth unapologetic. She was singing about Southern trees with strange, bloody fruit, bodies swinging in the breeze. She wore a checked cotton dress, and her hair was in nappy braids. Kids stared at her, hurried past, snickered. It didn't matter that her voice was rich and sweet as orange-blossom honey, Bee thought. It didn't matter that only the setting made her strange. On a stage in a long gold satin gown, under a few lights, she would have been purely stunning.

"Stunning," Bee said aloud, without meaning to. It was a relief to not think about the doppelganger for a moment; the singing had done that.

"Fat, however." The girl had stopped singing. Up close, her gorgeous lips were chapped. Her palms were pink against the dark of the rest of her skin.

"What?"

"I'm too big to be stunning."

"No you're not."

"It's the truth. I am. They won't sign you

if you're overweight. It wasn't that way in Billie's day."

"That was a Billie Holiday song, right?"

"Yes. She is my idol."

"And it's about lynching."

"That's right. How do you know it?"

"My mom and her boyfriend are very politically correct. They've been educating me in injustice since I was little."

"Bless them."

"I guess. I mean, it's good to know it all. I just think it verges on abuse when you tell a five-year-old about Hiroshima and Hitler and slavery."

"Yes, I suppose so. My family just ignores the whole subject. They would rather forget. I don't think you can."

"What's your name?" Bee asked.

"I'm Sarah."

"Hello. I'm Bee."

"As in honeybee?"

"Yes. Well, that's how I spell it. It was originally Beatrice."

"You're more a bee."

"Thanks. I think."

"Oh yes, it's a compliment. Bees are amazing. They have a queen, you know?"

"That's right," Bee said. "A queen."

Bee shivered in the heat as she said the word but she had no idea why. A queen. A girl who sang like an angel. An alien boy quoting poetry. A double. "Fetch" was another word for "doppelganger"; she'd looked it up last night. The name itself made her stomach lurch and her nape prickle. All these things fascinated and frightened her at the same time. She wanted to understand.

"I better get to class," Sarah said.

"Yeah. See you later."

Bee looked up at the jacaranda, imagining, among the clouds of purple blossoms and the ferny foliage, bodies hanging, pulpy as fruit, making the tree groan with weight and despair. She shivered again, wondering if the girl who looked just like her was hidden somewhere, watching. Had she really been there? And why had she come?

4

The Alien

Bee had hardly slept all night, wondering if the fetch would return.

What would happen then? Would Bee scream, run, call for her mother or just say "Hello, fetch. By the way, who are you and what the hell do you want?"

Finally she gave up on sleep and got out

of bed to bathe and drink some green tea. The silty, jade-colored liquid didn't calm her or bring her fully awake, and the air in the house felt stuffy. She had a sudden desire to be outside, near the ocean and away from the place she had seen the girl.

Bee passed wooden porches, fenced-in gardens with birdbaths, wicker chairs, clambering roses. She kept walking on the little paths, under the arcade of fake Italian columns, down the walkways where the little boys with sun-bleached dreadlocks set up their skateboard ramps. Eventually she got to the sea. It was usually overcast this early in the morning; the vendors hadn't set up yet and the boardwalk was still empty. People admired the palm trees, but Bee didn't quite get it; they looked ragged and sickly, out of place. Someone had imported them a long time ago. That was how she felt most of the time. Weirdly transplanted, though she had been in the same beach shack her whole life. She was even born there, her mother reclining on a pile of towels on the floor, a basin of hot water and a midwife at her side. But in spite of this, none of it felt like home.

She loved Deena in her way, but there was always this sensation of longing. As if another mother existed somewhere, like those women you heard about on the news whose children had been abducted in malls or parks, just vanished. Women who could do nothing anymore except wait to die.

Bee sat down on the dirty sand and scowled out over the gray water. She repressed an impulse to gather the chips of shell, put them in her mouth and crunch them to bits; pop seaweed pods and suck the salt; bury her body in the sand like a corpse in a sarcophagus. Sandpipers paraded up and down, and gulls shrieked. A rumpled, dirt-caked guy searched for coins with his metal detector. There were even a few surfers out there in their wet suits, long hair matted with salt, bodies shiny and sleek as seals. Sometimes you saw dolphins, but it didn't seem beautiful to Bee. Just sad, and sometimes, when the sun burned through so hot you could fry your skin in minutes, almost apocalyptic. But she felt safer here than at home somehow. Her doppelganger would never appear on a public beach like this, standing over Bee wrapped in windy strands of hair. Would she?

When Bee looked up, someone was standing there, watching her.

He was wearing a hooded sweatshirt and

squinting without his glasses so she hardly recognized him. Haze?

"What are you doing?"

"I stopped by your h-h-house. Your mom said you were at the beach. She told me which lifeguard stand you usually h-h-hang out at."

"You came to my house? At eight on a Saturday? How do you know where I live?"

"I hacked the school computer system. It's really easy."

"What? Why?"

He sat down next to her, looking out at the waves, not at her, hunched in his sweatshirt. He had long, awkward legs and he didn't seem to know where to place them.

"I just wanted to t-t-talk."

It figured Deena would have told him where she was. Her mother was always trying to get Bee to talk to boys, make friends.

Well, she'd done it in the last week, hadn't she? And he'd told her in the first few minutes of their conversation that death wasn't that bad.

Who was Haze? He could be anyone.

He was holding a skateboard; she hadn't seen him skate before. Her mother probably liked that; it made him seem cool. On the bottom he'd drawn a picture of a creature with big eyes, a Mohawk, long eyelashes and long, trailing fingers, like a sexy punk E.T.

"About what?" She wasn't going to trust him that easily. Just because he was an outsider like herself. With pretty eyes.

"I don't know. Not everyone talks to me about doppelgangers. You seem interesting. More than most people."

"Thanks." She frowned at him. "That's *quite* a compliment."

"You kn-n-now what I mean."

He turned to look at her profile; she could feel his gaze. Her hair whipped against her neck and shoulders. It just kept growing, was down to her hips now. And her eyes scared people. They were widely spaced, big and bright, with strangely large pupils. She was too skinny, no breasts to speak of. But men looked at her anyway, even when she dressed in baggy boy clothes. She didn't want men to look at her. It didn't help to be pretty, or whatever word you wanted to use. She was still unpopular, still a freak.

A freak with a twin—a fetch who visited her in the night.

"I gotta go home now," she said, getting up. He followed her.

"Have you seen her again?"

"Who?"

"Your doppelganger."

"Who says I saw one?"

"You did. B-b-basically."

"I was just asking you about it. For . . . something I'm working on."

"So, in this thing you're working on does the girl see her evil twin again?"

"No," said Bee. "Not yet. But I think she will."

Later they were on the boardwalk. It was more crowded now, Haze skating while she walked beside him, her arms crossed protectively over her chest. As if she were trying to prevent him having any further access to her heart. She didn't need the complication.

But: "Who's that face on the bottom of your board?" she asked anyway, in spite of herself. "An alien?"

He nodded. "A self-portrait."

"So you're an extraterrestrial?" It was a joke, of course, but his expression remained serious, drawn.

"M-m-maybe."

Why should she be surprised? She had seen her double standing at the window. Nothing was certain.

"So, what's your story?"

He kept skating while he talked, didn't look at her. The rough sandpaper sound of skateboard wheels on cement. "My mom was impregnated by one. He came in a spaceship and did it and left. That's how they plan to take over our planet."

"Take over the . . ."

"Yeah. I know. You asked."

She had asked. She turned off the board-walk through the alley that led back to her house. He followed her. Past the colorful old cottages with stacks of surfboards in front, their stained-glass windows and beds of shells and lilies; gardenias, dahlias and rhododendrons in Chinese cloisonné pots. He had put his glasses on again, to skate, but he didn't look like the kid from school. He was gracefully balanced on the board, hipbones showing through his T-shirt above the low rise of his jeans, baggy knees, chunky sneakers. Joseph Hayes was a hottie. Who knew?

She stopped at her gate and he hesitated; she could tell he wanted to come inside. But she wasn't going to let him. It was all too weird lately.

"Good-bye," she said, pulling the string that released the lock and stepping into the rambling garden. Sandy the golden met her at the gate, wagging, his mouth open in a perpetual smile. She could smell pancakes and syrup, scrambled eggs, sausages. Her mother's weekend extravaganzas. She hadn't felt like eating much lately, but she had an appetite now. The sun was just starting to come out, clouds moving to reveal the sea-blue color. The roses in Deena's garden were sugar pink against the pale green wall. Not everyone got to live with roses like that, got to walk to the ocean before breakfast.

Did this new way of seeing have to do with Haze? With the appearance of the girl?

Either way, something was different—what? Something was changing.

5

Fetch

The dream: She was walking down a sidewalk with a two-year-old girl. The child was round everywhere, with dimpled wrists and blond curls. She looked up at Bee with her round, lashy blue eyes shining above full pink cheeks you wanted to squish.

"Shoo-shoo," she said.

Bee knew what it meant. "You have to go shoo-shoo? Let's find a potty."

She turned her head, and the girl let go of her hand. When she looked back, Bee saw her sliding down through the sewer opening under the gutter.

Bee flung herself on her belly and slid down after her. There was a large, dark room with pipes lining the walls. She clung to the pipes, staring down into the shadows, calling for the girl.

There she was! Suspended by her arms on one of the pipes, like she was on a climbing structure at the park. Bee heard her say "Shoo-shoo" again and the stream of her pee on the cement below them. Bee swung along the pipes toward her.

"I'm coming, baby, don't worry."

But when she got there, she did not find

the child at all. Only a small doll swinging from the pipe.

The room was mostly dark, just a seashell night-light illuminating the tiny bathroom she shared with her mom and Lew. She was at the sink, splashing cold water on her face, trying to wash away the nightmare, the nausea, the pounding sensation in her head. A tapping sound and she looked up, into the mirror. She thought of that game they used to play when they were kids: "I believe in Mary Mack." If you said it into the mirror enough times you were supposed to see the witch Bloody Mary, who would scratch your face off and then you would die. Or maybe you would learn something important about yourself if you survived; who knew?

"I believe," Bee whispered, suddenly

wanting to understand, no matter how dangerous it turned out to be.

There was a long silence. Bee gripped the countertop, forcing herself not to run out of the room.

"You have my life," said a hazy light in the mirror. "Give it the hell back."

6

The Peculiar Institution

Stephanie," Sarah's grandmother called. "Is that you?"

Her name was not Stephanie. Sometimes she forgot that they still called her that and it took her a while to understand to whom they were speaking. This happened at school, all the time. *Stephanie; Stephanie*

Caldwell. And she just sat there staring at them so that they thought she was an idiot or on drugs.

There was no reason to be so unhappy, she reasoned as she threw her backpack on the couch. So they didn't understand her; so what? There were worse things. She lived in a pleasant house that her father had redone himself. Her grandmother took good care of them. Sarah was well fed. She always had the things she needed, although people thought she didn't because she refused to wear the dresses her grandmother bought for her, insisted on the cotton thrift-shop house-dresses instead. Yes, her mother had died, but it was so long ago she could hardly remember her at all.

So here she was, in for another night of homework and dinner—baked chicken, salad, potatoes, ice cream for dessert—reality TV. After that she might go online and study the Civil War, slavery, searching pictures of men with whipping welts like giant trees of flesh and blood on their backs. Searching slave girls from that time. Trying to find more about the one she had been.

It sounded depressing, but actually, it was strangely comforting. It was the only way she knew to find meaning, find out who she really was.

Today she had learned that some slave owners called slavery "the peculiar institution." Wasn't that the understatement of that century?

The worst part was the dreams. They were so real, unrelenting. The squeal of the hogs as the men slashed their throats, the hot smell of blood in the dust, the carcasses dangling upside down. The master who came to her at night, slipped into her bed, his clammy hands with fingers like giant maggots covering her mouth. Now, at last, she had someone to tell: that thin girl with the big eyes. Sarah somehow knew instinctively she would understand.

"Stephanie!"

"Yes, Gramma. I'm home." But no, not Stephanie. Stephanie wasn't.

Bee saw Sarah again on Monday, still singing her "Strange Fruit" song.

"Hello!" Sarah said, interrupting herself. "I've been thinking about you."

"Me, too," said Bee. "About you." At home she had played the original Billie Holiday version and thought that Sarah's was just about as good. It was amazing, really, that no one had discovered her yet, swooped down, scooped her up and put her on that crazy TV show where you had to sing in front of a panel of judges with personality disorders.

"Do you want to eat lunch?" Bee asked her. She had the distinct and novel knowing that she needed people around her now, as often as possible. Strange, strong people who understood her.

As if he had heard her thoughts, Haze walked up and joined them without asking, just slid onto the bench and sat there, not meeting their eyes.

"Hello," Sarah said.

"This is Haze," said Bee. "Haze, Sarah."

"Hi," he managed. He even looked up at them. His glasses were taped together in the middle.

"What happened to your specs?"

"S-s-some kids smashed them."

"You should have stopped them with your alien superpowers."

She could tell this hurt his feelings and she felt bad, but it was too late.

"Are you an alien?" Sarah asked. Perfectly serious and composed. She wasn't taunting him at all.

He seemed to relax a little.

"I'm actually a slave girl from the 1800s," she went on. "Reincarnated. Now, nobody seems to believe that, you know, but it doesn't matter; I know it is the truth."

Bee thought, My life just keeps getting odder every day.

"Now, B-b-bee here isn't freaky like us. Are you, Bee? Except that she sees herself walking around every once in a while. But that's n-n-normal."

"Okay. I get it. Sorry I said that."

He shrugged an acceptance to her apology. Sarah smiled at them. White, white teeth between her lush lips. "It looks as if we have found our kindred," she said.

A few months ago this would have been the answer to all Bee's problems, but things were different now. Not only the difference she had noticed that day when Haze surprised her at the beach, beauty revealing itself suddenly in ways she had never noticed before.

She hadn't told Sarah and Haze about the second encounter with the girl. Or about the latest thing that had happened.

In her bed that morning there was a wormy piece of wood with some yarn taped to the top and a piece of gray fabric tied around the bottom.

When Bee put on her sweatshirt to leave for school, she noticed that one cuff had been ripped off. Her gray sweatshirt, the one she always wore.

7

Invisible

For the last two weeks they had hung out together. The three of them. Haze and Sarah and Bee. They had their own table. No one bothered them anymore.

Sarah ate cafeteria food—French fries and grilled cheese sandwiches. Haze brought avocado on pita from home. Bee sipped a 7UP;

most food made her feel sick lately. Deena worried that she was losing weight, but Bee figured it was just a stage, maybe hormonal, or maybe she was just excited to finally have friends. When she looked at Sarah and Haze she saw halos of fuzzy blue light around their heads, their glamorous auras.

One day, Lindsey Carlisle came over with two other girls. Her blond hair and ice-cube eyes and symmetrical features. Big chest; little, belligerent butt. She paraded up to them and held out a piece of paper.

"Let's see, what do we have here? An invitation! To a party! But there's a checklist on the back. I better take a look at this. You can come to this party if you are good-looking. Uh, no. Popular? Double no. Not fat? One is fat. Not a freak or a candidate for worst dressed? Oops. Sorry. No invite."

Bee wondered why a cruel nature seemed to be a requirement of popularity. Even more than beauty, sometimes. It made no sense, but neither did most things.

"How about if you're mean and rude?" Bee heard herself saying. "Do you get to come then? Or is that only the hostess?"

Lindsey flipped her off and walked away.

"You go, girl," said Sarah.

"Yeah, we're all going."

"What?"

"To Lindsey Carlisle's party," Bee said. "And since when do you talk like a twenty-first-century girl?"

Sarah smiled. "Change is in the air."

It was all a matter of believing in things. Haze believed he was an alien. Sarah was the present-day reincarnation of a slave girl. Bee was—something, she wasn't sure what.

"We're more powerful than we think," Bee said. "We just haven't explored it yet."

"What does that have to do with Lindsey Carlisle's party?"

They were gathered in Bee's mother's gazebo with the tattered saris hanging from the splintery wood. It was a hot afternoon, no breeze in the silk.

"Have you ever wanted to be invisible?" Bee asked.

"Of course," said Sarah. "What child hasn't?"

"So let's do a spell. Even if it doesn't work, if we believe it enough we can walk in anywhere and no one will have the guts to mess with us."

"H-h-how do you figure that?" Haze asked. He was gazing at her steadily through his glasses the way he always did, as if she were something miraculous and frightening, like a cat that had started to speak.

"We'll be holding our invisible heads high. But we'll be subtle, quiet. They won't notice us. If we all believe it, it'll work."

Bee had another reason for wanting to be invisible. The more magical protection from unseen forces she could acquire, the better.

The night of the party they all wore black and stood in a circle in Bee's room. A black candle burned in the center. It smelled like melting licorice.

"What are we supposed to do?" Sarah asked.

"I don't know," said Bee.

"I have an idea."

The girls both looked at Haze.

"In physics, the only reason we can see something is because the atoms are vibrating slow enough. So if they started vibrating faster, we couldn't see it."

"Wow, you really are smart!"

Haze met Bee's eyes for a moment before he glanced down at the floor.

"But what are we supposed to do?" she asked.

"Maybe just stare at the flame and imagine your body as particles of light. Then imagine the particles jumping really fast." When he was talking about things like this, Haze never stammered.

"I think we should spin," Sarah said.

"Spin?"

"Yes. Spin around with our arms out. Like this." She turned in a circle. "If we go really quickly, it might speed something up in our particles."

"Okay," said Bee, "it's worth a try."

So they imagined themselves as fast-moving particles and they spun and spun while shadows from the candle flame danced on the walls like Balinese stick puppets in the hands of frantic puppeteers, and they laughed, too, until they fell dizzily to the ground, buzzing with light.

"We're ready," Bee said.

She realized when she saw that first one: Haze had never smiled in her presence before. It changed his whole face like a light had been turned on inside of him; it was like finding a light switch when you'd been fumbling around in the dark for way too long. That smile made you forget the things you were afraid of, like Sarah's singing did.

And like Sarah's singing, it made you want more.

Lindsey lived in a big, new house on the canals. By the time they got there, drunk kids were staggering off the porch to collapse on the lawn. The house smelled of beer. Boys and girls were making out on the leather couches; the stereo was blasting. Someone had thrown up on the floor. The smell made Bee's stomach lurch; she wondered why they had bothered to come at all.

She glanced over at Haze. He looked good in his black Levi's and black T-shirt, black skater shoes. Sarah had traded in her usual cotton dress for a black sweat suit, and her hair was up in a bun under a baseball cap. Bee could tell they were concentrating on being invisible, but she saw them both. It didn't seem like anyone else could, though.

They came in and found the keg, filled cups for themselves. Lindsey walked right by, clutching some older guy, drunk and laughing. If she noticed them, she didn't care. It was a little anticlimactic, actually.

"Let's dance," Sarah said.

"Don't you think they'll s-s-see that?"

"Not if we move quick enough."

She pulled a CD out of her sweatshirt pocket and put it in the stereo. Then she hit the light switch and started moving around the sunken living room to the Killers.

Bee joined her. Dancing always helped you feel more like yourself. Whoever that was, anyway. She grabbed Haze's arm.

"Dance with us."

She could tell he didn't want to. But he finished the beer in one gulp and put down the plastic cup. Then he started moving, steady and graceful, from the hips, as if he'd been doing this in his bedroom, practicing for this moment with her. Only the coolest boys danced and got away with it. He wasn't invisible at all. She couldn't see anyone else.

Some other kids joined them—mostly girls and a few drunken boys they'd dragged out there, and pretty soon the whole room was jumping with bodies. Lindsey should have been grateful they'd crashed her boring party, Bee thought, twirling in circles so fast that no one could see her as muscle and flesh over bone. All she was was light.

As they were leaving, someone pushed something into Bee's hand. She scanned the crowd, trying to see who had done it, but the person was gone.

It was a flower, small tubular purple blossoms clustered on a stalk, each one the size of a finger puppet.

Usually it was a nice thing to get a flower. No one had ever given her one before, except for the fancy bouquets from her mom on her birthday. But now, as she jammed the blossom into her pocket, chills were creeping up her back, cold fingers sheathed in petals.

She, Haze and Sarah had just stepped out the front door when Lindsey spotted them. They had been having too much fun to remember to keep up the spell. The dancing had been fun, too, but the speed with which their bodies moved to the music always reminded them of Haze's vibrating-particle theory.

"Party crashers!" Lindsey screamed, like a girl auditioning for a part in a B horror movie.

Five boys were at Lindsey's side in what felt like seconds. Bee took Sarah's hand, then Haze's hand, and started running.

They stopped in the shelter of some trees that dripped darkness from their branches like leaves. The water of the canal gleamed under the bridge, light from a greenish moon swimming on the surface like ghostly ducks. Bee closed her eyes and tried to imagine herself as vibrating particles.

And then—with the curse, or, in this case, blessing, of the unpopular, the unathletic, the overweight, the strange—they vanished like shadows into the spring night.

8

Flight

The friends sat on the hill of grass near the empty playground. They'd been up all night after Lindsey's party, too giddy to sleep, wandering the neighborhood. They'd told their parents they were staying over at one another's houses. All three families were so delighted that their wallflowers had plans on a Saturday night, they didn't question them.

An airplane flew low overhead from the nearby airport. You could see it perfectly, like a toy model of a plane, but it was so loud that you knew it was real. Even the airplane looked beautiful to Bee then. Weeks ago, it had been another sign of man's infringement of the natural world, or just an irritant.

In spite of the queasy feeling in her stomach that had kept her from eating much for days, in spite of the girl in the mirror, she still felt that sensation of wonder she'd experienced that day with Haze at the beach and when she first heard Sarah sing. It was almost all the time now, not just at the obvious moments like a sunset or when you saw a baby smiling. Haze and Sarah wore those weird halos around their heads and the early sunlight had a viridescent tint, reflecting from the grass, she guessed. Maybe she was just hungover from not enough sleep. No sleep.

The gazebo with the roof like a circus hat had a bunch of balloons still tied to it, remnants of some kid's birthday party. There were tiny little greenish white daisies and clover blossoms mixed with the grass under her butt. She plucked a clover and crushed it in her fingers, then sniffed the slightly acrid chlorophyll sweetness.

"I wish we could fly," Sarah said.

They both looked at her. She had applied lip gloss in the park rest room after the mocha frappucino from Starbucks, and her mouth was outrageously beautiful.

"We could if we wanted," said Bee.

"Now we can *fly*?"

"Yes. We were invisible. Why can't we?"

She stood up and spread her arms. Sarah got up, too.

Haze stared at them. The talking-cat look again. Bee had an impulse to kiss him.

She put out her arms like wings. "Come on. We can't do this without you."

He stood reluctantly, wiping his hands on his thighs. She could tell he felt foolish, was only doing it for her and Sarah.

"What are we supposed to do?"

"This!"

Bee took off, running down the grassy slope, yelling, feeling the breeze lifting her hair, whipping it against her face. Sarah followed her, then Haze, all of them screaming as loud as they could.

It felt as if they levitated—who knew? There was no one there to tell them it hadn't happened.

• • •

When they collapsed into a heap at the bottom of the hill they were out of breath, panting. Bee lay with her head on Sarah's warm stomach and her feet sprawled over Haze. Her belly hurt, but she didn't tell them. The yellowish glow of the world pulsed before her.

She put her hands into the pocket of the boy's black suit jacket she'd found in a thrift shop (the gray sweatshirt with the missing cuff freaked her out too much to wear now) and felt something there; she'd forgotten the flower.

"Look what someone gave me at Lindsey's party."

"Who was it?" Sarah grinned at her.

"I didn't see."

"A secret admirer?"

Haze was scowling at the plant. She didn't

like how worried he looked all of a sudden. She wanted to see the smile that changed his face so much, when you could get one out of him.

"It's a weird-looking thing," she said. "Do you recognize it, Haze?"

She handed over the crushed blossom. He examined it gingerly, pushing his taped glasses back up on his nose. "It's not a local plant. *Digitalis purpurea*. Foxglove. It's also called dead man's bells or witches' gloves."

"That's frightening," said Sarah.

Haze took the flower over to a trash can and tossed it in, then wiped his hands on the grass.

"Go wash your hands, Bee."

"Why?"

"Digitalis is a deadly poison," Haze said.

9

Hand in Hand

It was a stucco house with barred windows, off Venice Boulevard. Haze lived there with his parents, who were both middle school teachers. Luckily, not at the school he went to. He was already unpopular enough. His father taught math, would stand at the front of the classroom scratching his head so that dandruff snowed onto his shoulders. When he got upset, he stammered. Haze believed that even though he had black hair (no dandruff, thank you!) and the same speech impediment, he was not his father's son. He believed he had learned the stutter and that his hair color was from his mother. It made much more sense to him that his father was an alien who had abducted Haze's mom for the sole purpose of spreading his (its?) seed. He sometimes wondered why the alien had chosen his mother, though. She had been much thinner at the time, and her black hair was not yet streaked with gray. She was smart, too. Maybe the alien liked her large eyes that reminded him of his own species. She almost never took her glasses off, but the alien could have seen her eyes through his alien-viewing device while she was sleeping.

Haze imagined the abduction as sterile, anesthetized. His mother never felt a thing. So he hadn't been born out of pain, but there was exploitation, and no love, either. What did that say about him?

But, on the other hand, maybe his mother desired the alien. She wasn't that interested in his father. Maybe this had been her brief means of escape. Who knew? Stranger things had happened; they were happening now.

The birds of paradise outside Haze's window were huge, with leaves like shields and thick char-black weapon beaks. They seemed threatening to him—vicious, almost. Weren't these plants supposed to be delicate orange flowers that looked as if they once grew in some kind of Eden? He pulled down the dusty venetian blinds so that he wouldn't have to look at the violent birds. Maybe he would sleep now in the dust-mote-strewn dimness. His eyes stung and his head hurt from the all-nighter they'd pulled, but he didn't feel sleepy.

He was sitting on his twin bed, the one he'd had since he was a little kid. He even still had the *Star Wars* quilt, but he planned on flipping it over to the plain blue side if he ever had anyone over. In his lap was a book by Yeats. The poetry made him feel better. It made him think of her.

> *For he comes, the human child,*
> *To the waters and the wild*
> *With a faery, hand in hand,*
> *From a world more full of weeping than he*
>   *can understand.*

There was so much weeping now, Haze thought. Even in his own brief thirteen years.

The twin towers crumbling before him on the TV screen, and the war alone would have been enough to make him want to cry and never stop. He wasn't like the boy in the poem (except for his solemn eyes). There were no warm hillsides with lowing calves, no kettles singing him lullabies or cute little brown mice. No, there were angry birds of paradise tapping their black beaks on his window. There was a screaming kettle and frozen dinners in the tiny kitchen with the stained linoleum and cracked tiles. The waters were the Pacific Ocean off Venice Beach, so polluted that some days you couldn't even go in; the surfers got infections. The sea levels and shorelines changing from an overheated climate. Far away, the ice melting, and dying polar bears. And the wild was—what? The tangled beach garden he had glimpsed behind Bee's gate, burning up as the ozone thinned. But yes, there was weeping, just more of it. The weeping that spanned continents and generations. Sarah understood. She carried the weeping of a three-hundred-year-old practice like a scar on her back, as if it were happening today, and in some ways it was. Pain didn't ever really stop, he thought; it just changed forms.

And yet maybe there was a different "waters and the wild," somewhere hidden, farther than the eye could see. There was a girl who had taken his hand.

10

The Imposter

Deena was sitting at Bee's bedside when she woke late the next afternoon. She'd gotten home around ten in the morning and thrown herself down on the bed, still dressed, teeth unbrushed.

"Baby?" Deena said, stroking her tangled hair. "Bee?"

The light in the room made Bee's eyes hurt, and her stomach shook as if inhabited by some nasty goblin.

"What's wrong? Are you sick?"

"My stomach hurts," Bee said. "I feel like I'm going to vomit, but then I don't."

"We're going to the doctor."

"No, I'm all right. I think I'm just over-stimulated or something."

"Do you want to explain that one to me? Do we need to take you to buy some condoms?"

"Mom! No."

Deena felt Bee's forehead again.

"I'm okay, really. There's just a lot going on."

"Like what?"

What was she supposed to say? *I've been having visitations from my doppelganger. This boy I like thinks he's an alien. We got invisible together.*

Who knew? We flew. Yeah, right.

"Let me take your temperature."

But Bee jumped out of bed, ignoring the belly goblin. "I'm fine, okay? I just needed to rest. You worry too much."

"That's what mothers do," Deena said. "You'll see. But not any time soon."

"That's one thing you don't have to worry about."

Bee thought of Haze, his smile, how he looked at her. There were a lot of girls that were already having sex, but she knew she wasn't nearly ready. Would she ever be? She hadn't even gotten her period yet. She just wanted to be near him, listening to him recite poetry, maybe holding his hand, his eyes transforming her into something magical. It wasn't much different from what she wanted with Sarah.

But her friends wore halos. She had, if only

briefly, belonged. The world she had never loved before had turned to gold.

Under the ground seep the toxins of the population that lives above. If you have to, you will eat roots and earthworms. It is always night. Candles burn in lanterns made from tin cans. When it is nighttime up above, you can crawl out, but only for a little while. You feel ashamed of your matted hair, your torn clothes, the dirt on your face. Who would want to speak to you? They are all shiny and pretty. They have parents and houses with gardens. What do you have? The earth. Whole handfuls of it. The lizard people with their slit eyes and scaly skin. Your loneliness. Your longing.

The girl missed her mother in a monstrous way. She missed her with a fanged longing, a zombie ache. Not having her mother was like not having a soul. She was sure that she had a soul somewhere, but it did not feel that way. Maybe she did not have a soul at all. Maybe it had been taken along with her mother, along with her entire life.

The girl watched her mother as she slept. Her mother's mouth was a rosy bow, like the ones on top of the changeling imposter's birthday gifts.

The man lying next to the girl's mother had gray hair and needed a wheelchair to get around. He sat with the imposter in the garden and spoke gently to her. He valued what she had to say. Smiled proudly at her. Even though she was not related to him by blood, she was his.

The girl was nobody's. Except her mother's and her mother did not know it yet.

Now there were two other people that the girl needed to watch. One was a badly dressed overweight girl with dark skin and a musical voice. The other was a skinny boy with a stammer and broken glasses. The girl doubted she would have befriended these two outcasts. She imagined herself as one of the popular girls.

She turned and watched her mother sleep. She had an impulse to touch her olive-toned, lightly freckled skin, to smell her dark hair. She knew it would smell even more of lavender oil if she just leaned closer. . . .

But in the other room the imposter moaned in her sleep. And the girl slid out the open window, back into the wilder night, where she had never belonged.

test for a changeling

cook my dinner in an eggshell
see if i say a word
bathe me in foxglove poison
repeat the lord's prayer
place steel on my bedsheets
whip me drown me shove me in the oven
then you will see that i am not a piece of
    glamorized wood
not a sullen hairy beast with a venomous bite
    boils on my skin
blood between my legs
only a girl trying desperately to grow
into a woman

11

Test

In her dream, Bee was walking along a road that wound through a canyon. The eucalyptus leaves leaned down, silvery green and medicinal-smelling, trying to shelter her, kiss her or clutch her, she wasn't sure. Every once in a while a car sped by, dangerously close, blinding her in its headlights, and she pressed herself up against the dirt where wild evening primrose bloomed pinkish lavender by day, but now it was night and they slept gray in shadow. The ruins of an old castle crowned one ridge. The crumbling stone balustrades, balconies and cupolas, the foundation overgrown with weeds. She wandered up there, knowing this was the place, though not sure how she knew, or what place it was.

Among the castle ruins was a low stone bench covered with vines. These she knew to part like hair. She peeked through into an opening, a small tunnel just big enough for her to enter on her belly.

The earth smelled dank, and she heard the murmur of distant water. She slithered through the opening, down, down into the darkness.

"There you are!"

Bee turned her head so fast that her hair whipped her face. The strands felt sharp for a second, as if they weren't hair at all but little thorns. The doppelganger was standing in the shadows of the grotto room.

Bee crouched down on the dark stone floor and wrapped her arms around her legs. She could hear the soft rush of water that ran through the grotto. Her body shook like the eucalyptus leaves in the breeze of her mother's garden. But there was no real breeze down here.

The girl crouched beside her. Bee stared at the other face. Her own face. Fuller, though, and less strange. But the same. She remembered once seeing a photograph of twin girls, identical, but one looked pretty and the other grasping, hungry, demented, almost ugly. It was all in the details—an expression in the eyes, the way the smaller girl reached out to grip her sister's sleeve. For a moment Bee wanted to feel the girl's cheek. Instead, she brushed her fingers across her own. It was cool and soft to her dry fingertips, almost like the underside of a mushroom. Her fingernails were lined blackly with dirt, so thick with it they ached.

Then the girl spoke.

"People used to do things to changelings like you. Vile-tempered, ugly, old-looking little things all dressed up in good-girl manners and a pretty-girl glamour spell. Test you. Cook your meals in an acorn or an eggshell to see if you cried out, 'I never saw a meal cooked in an eggshell before, beer brewed in an acorn!' They frightened you with steel. You don't like steel, do you? Put an effigy of wood where you lay to curse you. Or you'd be whipped to make you confess. Then you would turn into your true self—a hideous elf that just lay there, not moving, drooling down your chin. If you didn't pass the test they'd make you drink water poisoned by witches' gloves. Or they'd drown you in the river. They'd shove you in the oven. Burn you to death alive. Mother is too nice; she'd never do such a thing, even if she knew the truth. You're lucky, because there are people who would. If they knew that it would make you disappear and bring their real daughter back.

"What say you, beastie? Can you pass the test? Does it make your skin crawl? Do you feel gnawed by rabid rodents? Will it kill you? Don't come crying to me, now, fetch. There's a simple solution to your worries. Give me back my life."

12

"Tiend to Hell"

Bee hadn't been in school for a couple of days. She didn't answer their calls or emails.

"I'm worried," Sarah told Haze at lunch. They were sitting together at their table, staring at the empty space where Bee usually was.

"I've been doing some research," he said.

"I think I understand what might be happening."

"What? You better tell."

"I think she's a changeling."

"A what? One of those fairy things they exchange at birth?"

He nodded.

"That explains why we all get along so well," Sarah said.

"And it also means someone wants her to go back where she came from."

Sarah tugged at her braids. "We should go see her."

So after school she and Haze went over to Bee's house. Lew answered the door.

"You must be Sarah. And Haze. I'm Lew."

"Is she all right?" Sarah asked. "We're sorry to just come by. We hadn't heard from her."

He asked them in. The house was small but

pretty. Bee's mom had painted the walls and furniture an unusual mix of colors. Lavender with green trim. Yellow with rose. Lots of beaded Indian cushions and Mexican folk art. Framed astrological charts on the walls. Crystals that caught and refracted the sunlight.

They sat on the purple couch. There was a framed black-and-white photo of Bee watching them from the top of a bookcase. She wasn't smiling, and her deeply set eyes looked haunted.

"She's in the hospital," Lew said. "Her mom is there now."

"What's wrong?"

"They don't know."

"Can we see her?" Sarah asked.

"I can check with Deena."

There was a silence so loud it echoed. Then Haze said, "We don't want to bother you. But we'd really like to go there now."

He was looking at the black-and-white picture of Bee so hard that he thought his glasses would shatter.

Sarah glanced over at him. He looked different to her. Grown-up, suddenly, in spite of his pimples and bitten fingernails. She had a sudden impulse to touch his hand.

Lew nodded. "I'll arrange it," he said.

"We think we know who you are."

She opened her eyes. The boy was sitting at her bedside. His hair looked bluish black. Like a crow's feathers. He wasn't smiling. What was he doing here? She had been dreaming that she'd had another visitor before, a girl, with the same bluish black glow to her skin, who sang her lullabies. Had it been a dream?

"B-b-bee?"

"Is that my name? What a weird name. I don't think that's my name at all."

"Do you know where you are?" he asked.

She wrinkled her forehead at him.

"A hospital, Bee."

"I'm not going. There's too much steel there."

"What's wrong with steel?"

"I just don't like it."

"Bee," he said. "I want you to listen. I've been doing some research, and I think I know what's wrong."

"Wrong. Wrong. Wrong. How do I know right from wrong? I come from a place where it isn't the same."

"Exactly. I think you're from someplace else."

"Under the ground," she said. "Where the roots take hold and everything ends but also begins."

"I think you're being poisoned."

Bee began to say the words with hardly a breath between them. "Bonnie she was and brewed beer in an acorn. Thus spake the lord of the castle. The Queen of Elphane has lost her daughter. A girl in a long green gown with roses for her eyes. We had something to ask of her and now pray tell where has she gone? To perish nimbly among the foxgloves, pretty maid?"

He put his hand on her wrist. There was a tube going into the vein in her tiny arm.

"If I'm right, I think you were exchanged at birth. They stole Deena's real daughter. And now that girl wants to get back. She'll do anything to get her life back. She's the doppelganger."

"Who?" Bee shrieked, thrashing in the bed, trying to sit up. "Who stole her away?"

A nurse peeked around the partition.

"Everything all right?"

Bee, quiet now, just stared at her.

"Visiting hours are almost over." The nurse looked stern.

He nodded and leaned in closer.

"They did. You know who they are. Better than I do. You know somewhere inside you. We have to remember. Maybe they can help us stop her."

She reached out with her free arm and touched his cheek. There were small red bumps there, as if his body were hurting itself from the inside out. Then she touched his throat where the Adam's apple protruded roughly. She watched it move up and down under the light graze of her fingers.

This comforted her, this touching. It was the only thing. But his touch was not for her. He was not hers. She thought of the girl with the beautiful voice. This boy and this girl were meant to be together and she, the one he called Bee—she was meant to go back somewhere. But where?

"Tell me something," she said. "Tell me something, strange lad with the crow's hair. Something to help me remember."

> "And pleasant is the fairy land,
>   But, an eerie tale to tell,
>   Ay at the end of seven years,
>   We pay a tiend to hell,
>   I am sae fair and fu o flesh,
>   I'm feard it be mysel."

"What? What's that?" Bee asked him.

"'Tam Lin.' The fairies have to sacrifice one of their own to hell every seven years. 'Tiend to hell.' Tam Lin was a prince who was captured by the Fairy Queen."

Bee looked around the room for the first time. The walls glowed yellow green, like a bruise. Everything was made of steel.

"'Tiend to hell,'" she said, looking into his eyes. "They sacrificed Tam Lin? Because he was fair? They wanted his eyes?"

"It's just an old ballad," the boy said.

"But what if I'm the tiend to hell? What if I'm the sacrifice?" Her eyes seemed to flare like candles about to go out. "What if this is hell?" she asked him. "Because I want to go back. To the other place, the place I belong."

"Maybe you've done the work you were supposed to do and the sacrifice is over," he said. "Maybe if someone loves you enough to let go of you, then you can go back."

13

The Journey

She woke and looked at the clock. It was three in the morning, the time when, she'd heard, people most often die, the time for spells.

Uranun caripe baglen ol
Gemeganza de-noan chiis gosaa

Zamicmage oleo lag-sapah arphe
Oresa ethamz taa tabegisoroch
Resa ethamz taa tabesgisoroch
Esa ethamz taa tabegisoroch
Zodinu ar zurah paremu
Zodimibe papnorge maninua
Zonac dodsih hoxmarch train
Amonons pare das niis kures

She bit down on her lip and ripped the tube from her arm, then pressed some gauze to stanch the blood. Surprisingly, she felt no pain.

She was still wearing the gown. It was a sickly green color and open in the back, exposing her rear end, so she took it off and went naked. It didn't matter. No one could see her. The invisibility spell had worked. It was easier not to make the unsightly gown invisible along with the rest of her, anyway.

She left the hospital.

She stood on the sidewalk in front of Cedars-Sinai. The sky was hazy with night fog. Not much traffic. Not much breeze, but she lifted her arms and closed her eyes. Now it was time for the second spell.

The city stretched below her, different than she had ever seen it. Beautiful, really. A grid of lights giving off a phosphorescent glow.

She flew north toward the shimmering hills, then east above Sunset. From this high up the billboards looked different, even huger. Giant boys and girls in designer sunglasses weren't just reminding her she could never be like them; now they were threatening to eat her alive. But they were so outrageously pretty, she wasn't sure she'd mind. She passed the fancy shops, the hotels, the record store, the restaurants, the night-clubs. Deena used to hang out here when she was a kid. A hippie born a little too late, coming of age when the kids were shaving their hair off and wearing swastikas instead of peace signs. Luckily, there were still remnants of an earlier time then; Deena had told Bee about having sprout sandwiches and hibiscus tea at a ramshackle place called the Source, seeing Cat Stevens browsing at Tower Records and Joni Mitchell holding court at the Rainbow. Now the Source was some cantina for hipsters, Cat Stevens was a Muslim named Yusef and Joni never left her house in Bel Air. Bee thought, What a strange place this is. If you made up a city like this, no one would have believed you. It seemed more like myth than reality—a whole metropolis built up around an industry that recorded dreams on giant screens, a city bordered by an ocean and a desert and snowcapped mountains. And right through the middle of the urban sprawl were canyons full of flowers, wild animals and secrets.

The French chateau on the corner was hidden behind a hedge, but you could see the peaked roof, especially from above. She landed softly and walked down the steep tiled driveway and entered, took the elevator to the lobby. No one stopped her—there were a few employees behind the desk—so the invisibility glamour must still be at work. She tiptoed over the carpet and down the steps into a room with high windows and lushly upholstered sofas. The color scheme was garnet and emerald. There were sconces on the wall, and the candlelight made the room seem haunted. She realized that the ghost haunting it was probably herself. Someone had left out a tray with a wine bottle and a glass, and a plate of fudge and strawberries. She poured herself a glass of wine and drank it. Immediately her head felt as if it was going to detach from her body and float away, so she stopped and ate a bit of chocolate instead. She realized then that she wasn't sick anymore. The symptoms she'd experienced in the hospital were gone. This was when she wondered if she was dead.

She vibrated with a chill and dropped a strawberry from her hand, then hurried out of the chateau and back out onto the boulevard. The night lifted her again, swirling her into the air like a leaf, and carried her farther east, and then north again into Laurel Canyon.

This was where she knew she was supposed

to be. The road was narrow, and the hills sloped up at a sharp angle on either side. Here were the eucalyptus of her dreams, the sleeping primroses. She flew farther into the canyon world until she came to a strange structure on the side of a hill.

It was a brick wall and stone balustrades—the remains of a grand stairway. Squat palms and jacarandas grew all around. She remembered her mother showing her this place before, and the queer chill she felt then, as a little girl, staring out of the car window.

"That's Houdini's mansion. The magician. It burned down in the fifties," Deena had said.

"Nineteen fifty-eight. His wife, Bess, said he came back to her during a séance," Lew had added. "And people see an apparition of a coach driven by white horses at Lookout Mountain Avenue."

"I knew he'd bring up ghosts," Deena said, in that eye-rolling way.

Lew just shrugged.

What would he think of his girlfriend's daughter now? At least he'd probably believe it, as opposed to Deena, who never would. Bee knew she should be missing them, but somehow she didn't. Was this what it felt like to be dead? She missed Sarah, though, and Haze. She remembered Haze sitting at her bedside in the hospital. Was that Haze? He'd only stammered once, and where were his glasses? He hadn't smiled—he was too worried—but she wished she had seen his smile one more time. Why couldn't her friends have come with her? The missing was an aching feeling in her chest, but dull, like when a part of your body goes to sleep. She realized the ache was in the exact space where her heart might have been beating. Maybe ghosts had to have longing or they wouldn't be ghosts; they'd just go away for good.

But there was another feeling inside her now as well. A sense that she had begun to love the world, finally, this alien world into which she had been thrown. Yes, she loved the world, with its Haze and its Sarah. It was no longer lonely. It was beautiful in its way, with its oceans and roses and light. But there was also the feeling that now, having met her friends, she had accomplished something, the thing, perhaps, she had come for: to touch their lives, to bring them together. Now she could go back to the place where she belonged. The balance had to be restored.

The bench. The one in her dream. She

knelt and ran her hands over the cool stone, the thick leonine legs wrapped with ivy.

Then she saw the opening in the side of the hill and she knew she was home.

progeny

the fairy queen knows these things
she has had long days and nights
indistinguishable
under the earth brooding about the
　　state of the world above

once she stood in a meadow and wept
because her revels had been interrupted
because of fire and flood
disease and death
still she had no idea how prophetic
　　were her words
the strange illness that poured
　　itself between bodies
through the elixir of the blood

wasting men before their time
their faces sunken and lumpy from the drugs
no immune systems to speak of and all
    because they loved

the queen's own husband had had his
    share of male paramours
it angered her enough to want
    to change the seasons
but she had sense not to destroy the world
the towers crumbling as the cards
    foretold they would
bodies flying from the windows like
    burning birds
that tsunami wiping out so many in its wake
the queen saved a young sylph put her in a tree
impressed with her lithe beauty
but the girl's beloved with his camera
    perished along with all the rest

what of the climate change? it
    terrified even the queen
a powerful sorceress witch and lesser deity
the ice melting the dying animals
    everything backwards
skin cancer more common now
    no ozone to protect

the queen once fair as milk cowered
    in her underground lair
avoiding mirrors and the realization
    of how she had changed
become a wizened monster
maybe it was better here
she no longer really missed the world
it was only her daughter
she needed

14

Progeny

Haze and Sarah were eating lunch together when they saw her. They knew immediately when she walked right past them. She did not even smile or say hello, but she did glance their way for a moment. Her eyes were completely different. The pupils that had made you want to jump inside them were now tiny pricks.

She was wearing new clothes—a pink tank top and pink camouflage pants. Her hair was freshly washed and pulled up in a high pony-tail. She wore makeup—mascara, lip gloss, blush on her cheeks.

A few nights before, Deena held her new daughter and wept with relief that she had recovered. Deena knew nothing of the change, but still she sensed it. This girl who snuggled in her arms had warmer, less translucent skin. She was less frail and less aggressively beautiful. Her breasts were starting to show. She sucked her lower lip like a baby so that her teeth protruded slightly. When did Bee start needing braces? Deena wondered. Even if Deena suspected something, she did not pursue it. She was relieved, deep down, that this new child had come to her. A real child.

One who needed her. A child of the world.

The girl walked right past Haze and Sarah and went to sit at Lindsey Carlisle's table.

"I miss her," Sarah said.

"Me, too."

"What happened?"

"I don't know." He lifted his fingers to his mouth, then dropped his hand in his lap. "She had to go back where she belonged."

"I thought she belonged with us."

"I know."

They were quiet for a while; it was too hard to speak about it. Plus, there was a part of both of them that wondered if they were wrong, if they were experiencing some kind of mutual delusion. It struck them, though, that whatever they were experiencing, they were not alone with it the way they had once been alone. Something had changed in both of them. It was as if they were seeing each other for the first time.

"I'm glad I have you, Alien Boy."

"You've got me." He could feel his chest tingle with the surprise of saying the words out loud to her. He never stammered anymore, and his mother had taken him to get contact lenses. He'd also gained a few inches, suddenly, almost overnight, so he towered above the other boys his age—above Sarah, now the tallest girl in their grade—and his skin was clearing up. It had started to get better the day after Bee had touched his cheek. Come to think of it, that was also when the stammering had stopped.

Sarah had changed, too. The dreams didn't haunt her anymore. Just yesterday, Haze had filmed her singing "Strange Fruit." They were going to send it in to *American Idol* for fun. In the video he'd made, she wore a gold satin dress that had been her mother's, and her grandmother had put waist-length braids in her hair.

One day, Haze and Sarah went to the park where they had once flown with their friend. They were close enough that they could smell each other, but they had not yet touched. His skin looked even paler beside hers. His hands were big. He could have covered her whole hand with his, made it disappear.

They were both beautiful. Neither realized that they had feared their own beauty, hid it intentionally. Neither realized they had been challenging the world: *Find me lovely anyway, desire my friendship, come close in spite of my strangeness, my belief in UFOs and reincarnation. I dare you.* But someone had come close anyway.

There was nothing left for them to prove.

"Are you really an alien?" Sarah asked him, turning her head to the side, wrinkling her nose. "Because you look like a young man to me."

"Are you Sarah?" he answered. "Or Stephanie?"

"Neither. I think I need a stage name."

"How about 'the Comeback Kid'?"

"Ha. What is that supposed to mean?"

"You know. Like you came back from another life."

"I thought that's what you meant. I'm okay being in this one now, thank you."

"Me, too," said Haze.

A cool low sea fog had chased all the children from the park. Night was coming, darkening the lawns. The sky was clear again now, a deep pulsing blue tinged with violet.

"Do you remember when we flew?" Haze asked her.

"Of course, young man."

Haze stood up, brushed the grass off his seat and held his hand out to her. His heart felt light and buoyant, as if it might lift him off his feet, an internal hot air balloon.

"Will you join me?"

"Are we leaving Planet Earth?"

"No, just taking a little trip. I don't want to leave anymore," he said softly, his new voice smooth as the evening sky.

Haze and Sarah knew that this was not the end of the world. At the same time, they sensed that perhaps the end of the world as they had known it was near. One of them had seen, or believed he had seen, whole galaxies destroyed and new ones reborn. The other had witnessed, or believed she had witnessed, unbearable human suffering and then returned to a world where one kind of suffering had been abolished, at least in certain places, and new suffering had come to pass. They both, in their short present lives, had known war and watched the climate change enough to threaten the earth's existence. They had found each other; they belonged to the world. They had lost Bee, but not forever. Under the earth upon which the dream city of Los Angeles had been built, they sensed a stirring as of water, a shining as of gold. They felt the reverberations of music. Magic had returned. The king and queen, having shed their old skins, reached out to embrace their lost child in an underground garden.

And her friends knew someday they would find her again.